Two of Everything

A Chinese Folktale

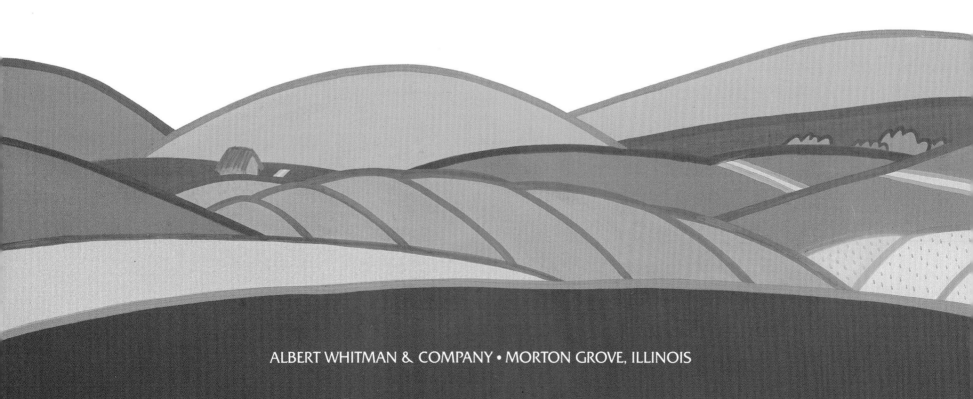

ALBERT WHITMAN & COMPANY · MORTON GROVE, ILLINOIS

Two of Everything

Retold and illustrated by Lily Toy Hong

Once long ago, in a humble little hut, lived Mr. Haktak and his wife, Mrs. Haktak. They were old and very poor. What little they ate came from their tiny garden.

In a lucky year when the harvest was plentiful, Mr. Haktak had a little extra to take to the village. There he traded turnips, potatoes, and other vegetables for clothing, lamp oil, and fresh seeds.

One spring morning when Mr. Haktak was digging in his garden, his shovel struck something hard. Puzzled, he dug deeper into the dark ground until he came upon an ancient pot made of brass. "How odd," said Mr. Haktak to himself. "To think that I have been digging here all these years and never came upon this pot before! I will take it home. Maybe Mrs. Haktak can find some use for it."

The pot was big and heavy for old Mr. Haktak. As he stumbled along, his purse, which contained his last five gold coins, fell to the ground. He tossed it into the pot for safekeeping and staggered home.

His wife greeted him at the door. "Dear husband, what a strange pot!" Mr. Haktak explained how he found the pot. "I wonder what we can do with it," said Mrs. Haktak. "It looks too large to cook in and too small to bathe in."

As Mrs. Haktak leaned over to peer into the pot, her hairpin—the only one she owned—fell in. She felt around in the pot, and suddenly her eyes grew round with surprise. "Look!" she shouted. "I've pulled out TWO hairpins, exactly alike, and TWO purses, too!" Sure enough, the purses were identical, and so were the hairpins. Inside each purse were five gold coins!

Mr. Haktak was so excited he jumped up and down. "Let's put my winter coat inside the pot. If we are lucky again the pot will make two coats, and then we will both stay warm." So into the pot went one coat—and out came TWO coats.

They began to search the house and quickly put more things into the magical pot. "If only we had some meat," wished Mr. Haktak, "or fresh fruit, or one delicious sweet cake."

Mrs. Haktak smiled. "I know how we can get anything we want," she said. She put their ten coins into one purse, then threw it into the pot. She pulled out two purses with ten coins in each.

"What a clever wife I have!" cried Mr. Haktak. "Each time we do this we will have twice as much money as before!"

The Haktaks worked late into the night, filling and emptying the pot until the floor was covered with coins.

Morning came, and off went Mr. Haktak with a long list of things to buy in the village. Instead of vegetables, his basket was full of gold coins.

Mrs. Haktak finished all of her chores and sat down to enjoy a cup of tea. She sipped her tea and admired the brass pot. Then with a grateful heart, she knelt and embraced it. "Dear pot, I do not know where you came from, but you are my best friend." She stooped over the pot to look inside.

At that very moment, Mr. Haktak returned. His arms were so full of packages that he had to kick the door open. Bang! Mrs. Haktak was so startled that she lost her balance and fell headfirst into the pot!

Mr. Haktak ran over and grabbed his wife's legs. He pulled and tugged until she slid out onto the floor. But when he looked at the pot again, he gasped. Two more legs were sticking straight out of it! Naturally, he took hold of the ankles and pulled.

Out came a second person! She looked exactly like his wife.

The new Mrs. Haktak sat
silently on the floor looking lost.
But the first Mrs. Haktak cried,
"I am your one and only wife!
Put that woman back into the
pot right now!"

Mr. Haktak yelled, "No!
If I put her back we will not
have two women but THREE.
One wife is enough for me!"

He backed away from his
angry wife, and tripped and fell
headfirst into the pot himself!

Both Mrs. Haktaks rushed to rescue him. Each grasped an ankle, and together they pulled him out. There were two more legs in the pot. So they pulled out the other Mr. Haktak, too.

"Just what use does one Mr. Haktak have for another!" Mr. Haktak cried angrily. "This pot is not as wonderful as we thought it to be. Now even our troubles are beginning to double."

But his wife had been thinking while he was yelling.

"Calm down," she said. "It is good that the other Mrs. Haktak has her own Mr. Haktak. Perhaps we will become best of friends. After all, we are so alike he will be a brother to you and she a sister to me. With our pot we can make two of everything, so there will be plenty to go around."

And that is what they did. The Haktaks built two fine new homes. Each house had identical teapots, rice bowls, silk embroideries, and bamboo furniture.

From the outside the houses looked exactly alike, but there was one difference. Hidden in one house was a big brass pot. Of course, the Haktaks were always very careful not to fall into it again!

The new Haktaks and the old Haktaks did become good friends. The neighbors thought that the Haktaks had grown so rich that they decided to have two of everything—even themselves!

For Kellan

LILY TOY HONG lived most of her life in Salt Lake City, Utah. She grew up in a large Chinese-American family, the seventh of nine children. She says she always knew she wanted to write and illustrate children's books.

Ms. Hong is married and lives in Murray, Utah, where she hopes some day to find a magic pot in her backyard. *Two of Everything* is the second book she has written and illustrated. Her first book is *How the Ox Star Fell from Heaven.*

Illustrations in airbrushed acrylics and gouache.
Text type set in Fritz Quadrata.
Calligraphy by Robert Borja.
Designed by Karen Johnson Campbell.

Text and illustrations © 1993 by Lily Toy Hong.
Published in 1993 by Albert Whitman & Company,
6340 Oakton Street, Morton Grove, Illinois 60053.
Published simultaneously in Canada by
Fitzhenry & Whiteside, Markham, Ontario.
Printed in the United States of America.
20 19 18   17 16 15

Library of Congress Cataloging-in-Publication Data
Hong, Lily Toy
Two of everything/retold and illustrated by
Lily Toy Hong.
p. cm
Summary: A poor old Chinese farmer finds a magic
brass pot that doubles or duplicates whatever is
placed inside it, but his efforts to make himself
wealthy lead to unexpected complications.
ISBN 0-8075-8157-7
[1. Fairy tales. 2. Folklore—China.] I. Title.
Pz8.H722Tw   1993   92-29880
398.21—dc20   CIP
[E]   AC

To learn more about Albert Whitman & Company,
please visit www.albertwhitman.com.

A